LIONEL PRIMARY SCHOOL
LIONEL ROAD
BRENTFORD, TW8 9QT

First published in Great Britain in 1991
by Simon & Schuster Young Books
This edition published in 2001 by Hodder Children's Books

10 9 8 7 6 5 4 3 2

A Catalogue record for this book is available from the British Library

ISBN 0 340 79520 4

Printed by Wing King Tong, Hong Kong

Hodder Children's Books
A Division of Hodder Headline Limited
338 Euston Road, London NW1 3BH

JOAN AIKEN

The
SHOEMAKER'S
BOY

Illustrated by ALAN MARKS

Hodder
Children's
Books

a division of Hodder Headline Limited

Chapter One

Once there was a shoemaker's son called Jem. He lived with his parents in a small cottage and worked hard, learning his father's trade, making and mending all kinds of shoes.

But Jem was still young, nothing like so good at the craft as his father, when a trouble came on the family. Jem's mother fell dreadfully ill, and no doctor seemed able to help her.

Day after day she lay asleep on her bed, white as bread, hardly breathing, unable to eat solid food. Jem and his father were afraid she would die. She never spoke, never stirred. Nothing would rouse her.

Jem's father decided to walk all the way to the Holy City of St James, to pray that his wife might get better.

"If St James can't help her, nobody can," he said. "You be a good boy now, Jem. Look after her as well as you can. And try to keep the customers satisfied."

Jem was worried about this plan, for his father was the best shoemaker in three kingdoms. People came from far away to have him measure their feet and make them boots or shoes. How would Jem ever manage on his own?

But he swallowed, and nodded, and waved a cheerful goodbye to his father, who stuck a cockle-shell in his cap and walked away southwards, along with a party of pilgrims who were on their journey to the Holy City of St James, hundreds of miles distant.

Weeks went by
and months went by.
Jem did his very best,
making and mending
shoes for the customers.
Most of them were friendly
and didn't ask too much, knowing
about the family trouble. But, just the same,
Jem longed for his father. Money grew
short, he was falling further and further
behind with his orders, for he could not work
as quickly as his father, nor do as much, on
his own, as the two of them had done
together. Half-finished pairs of shoes lay all
over the cottage.

One evening Jem stepped outside for a quick breath of air, after giving his mother her supper – milk and honey, which was all she would ever take, and that no more than a spoonful – when he heard some faint, shrill, twittering voices behind him, and turned round to see three strange little children.

Were they children? They had wizened little faces, and thin, stick-like little arms and legs, and they came up no higher than his waist. They were all dressed in green.

"What did you say?" Jem asked, looking at them in surprise, for he had never seen anything like them before. Where in the world could they have come from?

"If you please, master, we have come for the three silver keys."

"Keys, what keys?" said Jem, very puzzled. "I have no silver keys."

"But, if you please, master, we were sent to ask you for them. The three silver keys. They were to be left with you. And we were to get them."

Jem shook his head, even more puzzled. "No one said anything to me about three silver keys. You must be wrong. And where in the name of goodness did you come from, you queer little beings?"

But when Jem said *"in the name of goodness"* the three rickety little creatures disappeared, vanished clean away – phttt! – just like that!

Jem rubbed his eyes, and rubbed them again.

"I must have dreamed them," he said to himself. "I'm tired, very tired – that's all."

He had good reason to be tired. For, night after night these last weeks, he had sat up, watching over his mother, feeding her a spoonful of milk every hour.

Chapter Two

That night he worked late, and was about to lie down on the cobbler's bench for half an hour's rest, when there came a loud bang on the door.

"Bother! Maybe it's those three children back again," thought Jem, not at all pleased at being disturbed. He was in no hurry to answer.

But the knock came again – thump, thump! – very sharp and impatient. It sounded too strong and rough to be the children. So Jem sighed, rubbed his eyes and his face, crossed the room, and unbarred the door.

Outside stood a knight. In the dusky light,
Jem could just see that he was dressed all in
black – over his armour he wore a black
tunic, and his shield and helmet were of
black metal, his cloak was black, and so was
the great horse that stood behind him,
steaming and stamping and shaking its
head.

"Hey, boy! I want you to make me a pair of boots," said the knight. "I have heard that the footwear you make here is the best in the land."

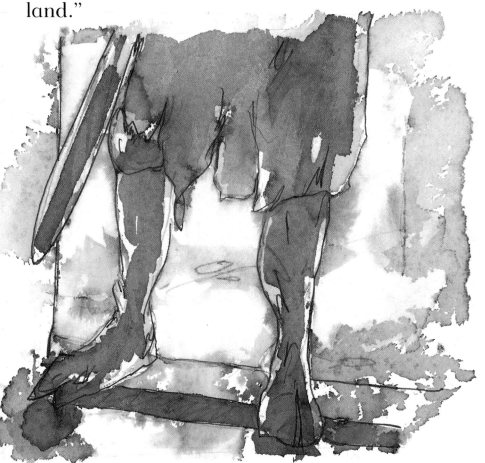

"Oh sir, but I'm afraid my father is away from home," said Jem. "I may not be able to make them as well as your honour wishes."

"You look to me like a clever boy, as well as a truthful one," said the knight. "I'll take a chance, for I have travelled a great distance to come here."

Indeed, when the knight walked inside, and Jem had lit a candle, he could guess that this must be so; the knight's cloak and tunic were worn and dusty, and the boots he wore were split and cracked.

Jem knelt to measure the knight's feet. He was too polite to exclaim, but the shape of them surprised him greatly; he had never seen such feet before in his whole life. And, by now, Jem had measured a great many feet.

"What is your price for a pair of boots?"
said the knight.

"One guinea, sir."

"I will give you two. But the boots must be
finished by breakfast time."

Jem thought that if he worked all night he
could just about manage this. And two
guineas would buy enough milk and honey
to last his mother for weeks, besides leather
and firewood and candles and thread and
shoemakers' needles.

"I will do my best to have them ready for you, sir," said Jem, hurriedly reaching for his shears to begin cutting the leather.

"The boots must be black. Oh, and by the way," said the knight, very carelessly, as he turned to leave, "I think three silver keys have been left here for me? You might as well give them to me now."

Outside the door, the knight's black horse let out a shrill neigh; the sound was so loud and sudden that it brought Jem's skin out in goosepimples.

"No, sir," he said. "I'm afraid you are wrong. Nobody has left any keys with me."

"No? Perhaps they will have before I come for the boots. Keep them for me carefully."

And the knight strode out. He did not say goodbye. And Jem felt a great deal more comfortable when he had gone, and the sound of his horse's hoofs had died away.

Chapter Three

That night, Jem worked harder than he ever had in his life before, cutting and snipping, stitching and stretching and shaping. One candle burned clean away, and he had to light another; still, never mind, the black knight's money would pay for plenty of candles.

One boot was finished, and the other well begun, when he heard another knock at the door.

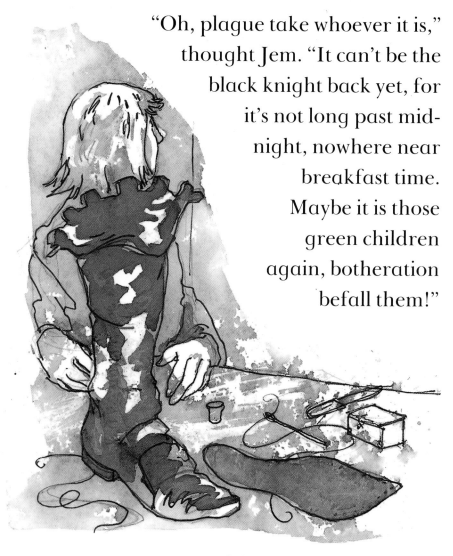

"Oh, plague take whoever it is," thought Jem. "It can't be the black knight back yet, for it's not long past midnight, nowhere near breakfast time. Maybe it is those green children again, botheration befall them!"

He called out, "Please go away, whoever you are! I'm very busy."

But a soft voice answered, "I promise I will take no more than a moment of your time."

Something about the voice made Jem think of his father. It certainly did not belong to those queer little children. So, rather impatiently, he unbarred the door again and looked out.

The moon was up now, and by its light he could see a white knight standing on the path. His cloak and tunic were white, his armour was of silver, so were his sword and the helmet that hung on his shoulders. On his shield Jem could see a crest showing three keys.

"Good evening, Jem," he said. "I am sorry to disturb you at your work, but I have heard that you are a good and trustworthy boy. I have come to ask a favour of you. You see this little packet? I need to leave it in a safe place while I go on an errand. May I leave it with you? And you will make sure that nobody, nobody at all, takes it or touches it?"

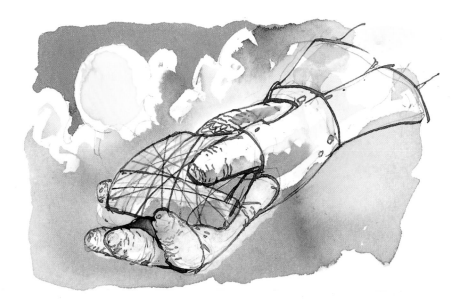

The knight handed Jem a small square of folded white silk, about the size of a purse, tied across and across with dozens of threads.

"Why, certainly, sir," said Jem, puzzled but polite. "I'll keep it carefully for you, if you wish. It shall go up here, on my top shelf. And I will see that no one touches it. But when will you be back for it?"

"If I am not back by daybreak," said the knight, "you may keep the packet. Good night to you now." And he sprang on to his white horse, which bolted away with the speed and silence of lightning.

Jem put the packet on the shelf, relocked the door, and went back to work.

Now he was very tired indeed, and found it harder and harder to set his stitches. His head nodded, and, what was worse, he thought he kept hearing voices. He heard the voices of the green, shrivelled children, wailing and squeaking outside the door.

"Let us in, Jem! Let us in to sit by your fire! We are perished with cold, Jem, we are hungry and freezing. We need those three keys, we need them dreadfully – let us in, please, please, let us in and give us the keys!"

"I have no keys for you!" Jem shouted, waking himself out of his dream, and he set to work again, harder than ever.

Then he thought he heard the black knight, riding round and round outside the cottage; and he heard the black horse stamp and snort and whinny.

"You had better give me those keys, Jem," shouted the black knight.

"I can't do that, sir. I promised that no one should touch them."

"Fool boy! Those keys were left there for me!"

Jem shook himself and trembled as he
thought he heard the horse whinny again.
And then he heard what sounded like a wild
battle: there were thumps and clangs and
bangs, shouts and blows and screams, the
neighing of several horses and the trample
of many hooves.

"Whatever is going on out there is no business of mine," thought Jem. "My business is to get this boot finished." And he ducked his head over his work, stitching and stitching away for dear life.

Once or twice he went to see how his mother did, in the back room, wondering that she was not roused by the sounds outside; but no, she lay as before, in her deep, strange sleep.

Chapter Four

Just before daybreak the second boot was done. "They are by far the best boots I have ever made," thought Jem, looking at them with pride as they stood side by side on the bench, soft and supple, finely stitched, and gleaming with polish.

Now there came a crashing thump on the door; the bolt broke and the door swung open. There stood the black knight, looking blacker than ever against the slowly growing light of day. He was all dusty and bleeding, his armour hacked and gashed, his shield was scratched and dented, so was his helmet, through the bars of which his eyes gleamed angrily.

It was plain that he had been in a fight, and, by the look of him, had had the worst of it.

"I've come for my boots, boy," he snapped. "Are they ready?"

"Yes, sir, quite ready," said Jem, and pointed to them, standing on the bench.

The knight tossed two gold coins on to the floor. He said, "And I'll have those keys, too."

"I have no keys for you, sir."

"Don't lie to me! The white knight left three keys for me, in a silk packet. There they are – on the shelf. It was for me he left them!"

The knight stepped forward to snatch the packet from the shelf, but Jem was before him, whipped them away, and sprang to the back of the shop, where he stood holding the little silk square, with its criss-cross of thread.

"Give it to me!" hissed the knight, through the bars of his helmet. "Take off that cursed wrapping and give it to me! Or I will slice your head clean off."

"No, sir. I have no right to give it to you."

The black knight moved forward a step, pulling his sword from the scabbard – and, just at that moment, the old rooster, perched on the roof above, crowed *cockadoodledoo!*

Jem saw the pair of black boots he had made wither and shrivel away like burnt paper in a blaze. Looking above the boots he saw that the black knight, too, had vanished clean away. And so had the gold guineas.

Nothing was left but the little white packet that he held in his hand.

"Well," thought Jem, "the white knight did say that, if he was not back by daybreak, I might keep the packet. And the sun has risen. So I may as well open it and see what is inside."

Very carefully he snipped through all the
threads that tied the packet, across and
across. Then he undid the white silk
wrapping. He had expected to find three
silver keys; but no, he found only a little
square of thin, soft white bread. Quite fresh
it seemed, considering that it had been
wrapped and tied up so tight for who knows
how long.

"Jem!" came his mother's voice faintly through the door. "Jem? I'm hungry, Jem!"

"*Mother!* Are you feeling better?"

Jem was thunderstruck, for it was months since his mother had spoken.

"I'm so hungry," she said, faintly stirring. "Oh, how I would like to eat a little piece of fresh white bread . . ."

Chapter Five

Two months later, Jem's father came home –
thin, worn, weary, footsore, grey-haired,
with his clothes frayed and torn and tattered.
But, my goodness! how happy he was to see
his wife strong and active and pink-cheeked
again, and to find how well his boy Jem had
managed, making and mending shoes and
boots, keeping the customers satisfied,
during the long months of his absence.

And, when they asked him – "Yes!" he said. "I got to the Holy City of St James. What a place! A main square the size of a town, and a church the size of a whole forest. I begged and prayed the saint to help us – and see how quickly he answered my prayer!

"But there was one moment, on the way, when I thought I should never reach the city, or see either of you again. For a band of brigands, led by a wicked fellow in black armour, set on our party in wild mountain country, and they would have killed us all if we had not been rescued, at the very last minute."

"Who rescued you, father?"

"A knight, all dressed in white. He was the best fighter I've ever seen – finished off half a dozen of the robbers, and the rest turned round and ran for their lives.

The knight wouldn't even stay to be thanked – said he had another errand, a long way off, and he galloped away before we could even find out his name. But the crest on his shield showed three keys . . ."

The Jewel Seed
Illustrated by Peter Bailey

The Jewel Seed is a powerful source of magic – used for both good and evil. But it's lost. No one knows where. Only Nonnie holds the key. Can she unravel the mystery before her worst enemies, a group of Siberian witches, catch up with her?

Fog Hounds, Wind Cat, Sea Mice
Illustrated by Peter Bailey

The Fog Hounds are mysterious – and deadly. They roam the land from dusk to dawn. No one who is chased by them ever lives to tell the tale. But Tad is not afraid. Tad wants one for himself. And when he comes face to face with a Fog Hound puppy, things can never be the same again.

For older readers:

Moon Cake and Other Stories
Illustrated by Wayne Anderson

"Witty and entrancing . . . Joan Aiken is one of the most remarkable writers in modern children's fiction." THE SUNDAY TIMES

HODDER

These colour story books are short, accessible novels for newly confident readers

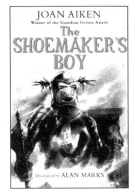

JOAN AIKEN
Winner of the Guardian Fiction Award
The SHOEMAKER'S BOY
Illustrated by ALAN MARKS

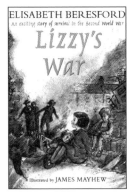

ELISABETH BERESFORD
An exciting story of survival in the Second World War
Lizzy's War
Illustrated by JAMES MAYHEW

ELISABETH BERESFORD
The exciting sequel to LIZZY'S WAR
Lizzy Fights On
Illustrated by JAMES MAYHEW

LEON GARFIELD
Winner of the Whitbread Children's Book Award
Fair's Fair
Illustrated by BRIAN HOSKIN

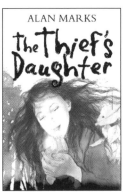

ALAN MARKS
The Thief's Daughter

MICHAEL MORPURGO
Winner of the Smarties Prize
THE KING IN THE FOREST
Illustrated by TONY KERINS

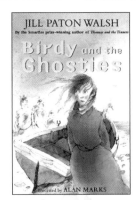

JILL PATON WALSH
By the Smarties prize-winning author of *Thomas and the Tinners*
Birdy and the Ghosties
Illustrated by ALAN MARKS

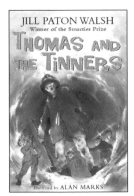

JILL PATON WALSH
Winner of the Smarties Prize
THOMAS AND THE TINNERS
Illustrated by ALAN MARKS